Immortal Illness

Emilia Sayaka Sarajlija

© 2022, Emilia Sayaka Sarajlija
Publisher: BoD - Books on Demand, Stockholm, Sweden
Print: BoD - Books on Demand, Norderstedt, Germany
ISBN: 978-91-8027-518-7

Day 3650: Wow, I've been writing these silly diaries for ten whole years now. Yay, I guess… I don't usually go through the things though, since they're just inner thoughts about my illness, but maybe I should reread some of it. My mother recommended it, since all my current thoughts are basically in shackles right now. I'm stuck with my chronically depressed ways of thinking and cannot find any means out of this, so what's the point, honestly? And insomnia, on top of that. I know, even I think I'm too bothersome for this world. Right now, the only thing keeping me alive is… well, that's a good question. What am I living for? I'm 21 years old, living alone, unemployed, single, with no social life except some vague contact with my mother over the phone (and my imaginary friends), I don't have any talents… Yeah, you get the hint. I'm not taking any antidepressants or sleeping pills anymore, as they don't affect me, so I need to keep filling these pages to keep myself sane.

"I think that's enough writing for today", I casually say out loud to myself while putting my diary away, but not hiding it. Maybe my imaginary friends want to read it, who knows. Azalea and Aconite are like the little sister and big brother I never had. Imaginary or not, they're my all. I even named them after flowers because of my love for the cute things. Azalea got the name because she is very gentle and loving, while Aconite got his name from his kind of toxic personality, though he always means well in the end. "I hope you'll find your meaning someday then," a sweet voice from nowhere tells me. It's the innocent little Azalea. Seems like she has been sitting beside me the whole time I was occupied with the diary, while Aconite was chilling out in my bed. He makes a comment about being impressed how I've dedicated myself to writing every day for 10 years. "Thanks, you two... I don't know if I'll have a happy ending, but I suppose I'm not writing in vain," I respond, mentally exhausted as usual. It is embarrassing that I've kept these guys by my side for longer than the average child. I'm an adult now: Aren't imaginary friends supposed to vanish at, what, 12 years old? Well, my friends stayed, and they have been the most loyal people in the world to me. It's safe and comfortable in my bubble, so I don't see a reason why I should be taking a needle and make an exit for myself. I don't want to lose Azalea and Aconite anyways. If there is something I'm really living for, it's them.

"What do you want to do, now that you've written the daily stuff down?", Aconite asks from the bed. His appearance is very bad boyish, with a black leather jacket and ripped jeans that matches his image. He decided to dye his hair from brunette to black and pierce his ears, even. Maybe to match everything else. He basically looks like he belongs in a motorcycle gang... If he was real, anyway. He hates when I call him 'big brother' instead of his actual name though. I don't know what's up with that, but whatever.

"We should play a game! That sounds fun, doesn't it?", the childish Azalea makes a remark and starts looking around my awkwardly furnished room for inspiration. Azalea is pretty much the opposite of Aconite: Beautiful, cheery and fragile in both character and appearance. She is very petite and loves her baby blue clothing, which is a light blue blouse with a longer white skirt. She usually has her dark blonde hair put up in a neat bun or ponytail.

"As long as it's not a shitty game, I'm in," Aconite says without giving any thought to the fact that I don't like when he swears.

"Stop the swearing already, Aconite. And I'm too tired to play any games, Azalea. Sorry. I just... wish I could fall asleep already," I say pessimistically while going to the small kitchen. I'm way too skinny because my source of energy are these forsaken snack bars. I'm not good at cooking, so I usually just let mom cook my meals when she comes over for a visit. The thing is, I don't like having people here, other than Azalea and Aconite. I can hear the two of them bickering in the other room, as they sometimes do like actual siblings, so I decide to stay in the kitchen and rest my head on the round, tiny dinner table. "This chair is uncomfortable, but it'll do for a quick nap." I slowly close my eyes and begin to drift away.

I wake up on the floor in a strange-looking hall somewhere unknown. I have no idea where I am nor how I got here. Didn't I just fall asleep? I sit up and look around. There are no doors or windows anywhere; it's simply a long, bright hallway. It's giving me claustrophobic vibes.

"… Hello?", I call out in hope for an answer, but all I hear is my voice echoing back, as if slapping me in the face. I realize this is probably a dream and lays back down, waiting it out. In an instant, I'll be gone from this creepy place. As soon as I begin to return to reality, a noise awakens me, disturbing me from getting back to Azalea and Aconite. A noise I'm all too familiar with.

"Hello?" I repeat myself in the direction where I can hear the desperate sobbing, but I don't see anyone. Strange. But then, when I turn my head back, two eyes meet mine. Pitch black orbs are staring right at me. It's a little girl with horizontal white-and-black stripes, with no other features than her short-length black hair, with bangs hanging all the way down over her eyes.

"Hello," she greets me. Her voice sounds young and adorable but tragic, as if she's been through something horrible just now. "I need help." She continues. "Can you save me?"

I don't know what to do, since I have to save myself from this dream. Oh, I forgot: This IS a dream, so why am I even listening to this girl? "Sorry, but I'm getting out of here," I tell her. I try not to come across as too harsh, but I don't care. It's a dream, dummy.

"... You're not going to help me?", the little girl asks. She suddenly sounds angry, as if her sadness got replaced with anger.

"No," I answer while touching the walls, trying to find an exit or a hole or... something. Anything to get me out.

"Then I won't help you," The now furious girl says while raising her voice and running straight towards my mouth, opening it forcefully and taking my tongue in her tiny hands, dragging it so hard that it feels like it's coming off.

"Ihh hurs... stahp...!" I shriek out, begging her with my deformed words to stop. The pain is excruciating. Soon, I begin to fall into a cold slumber.

"AAHHH!", I scream, and Azalea and Aconite comes for my rescue right away. They both shake me, asking me frantically if I'm okay. "What happened to you?!", Aconite screams back while taking a hold of my shoulders. I decide to stay silent, cover my mouth and think to myself, 'what in the hell just happened?'

"Are you feeling calmer...?", Azalea shyly asks me. I told them everything that happened in the dream, and I know it was a dream, but it hurt so much when that... thing... took my tongue and twisted it until I even tasted the blood coming up from my throat. Aconite was angry, for sure. He wanted to kill the girl for doing that to me. Not like he'd manage to sneak into the dreams and do it, but yeah. Azalea just felt bad for me for having such a 'grotesque' dream, as she phrased it.

"My tongue still hurts a bit, but I'll be fine. Thanks, guys."

"Of course. We'll always be here for you," Azalea reassures me with her usual innocent smile. I honestly hope so; I don't want to lose them, ever.

"Hey, Azalea?"

"Yes?"

"Let's grow old together, the three of us."

"I'm glad you didn't forget about me!". Aconite adds himself into the conversation, but we decide to tease him by ignoring him, going on about 'girly things'.

"H-hey! Don't ignore me!"

"Yes, yes, brother," I tease him further. He starts blushing slightly, but I don't know why.

"Don't call me 'brother'…", he mutters to himself.

"Come on, give me a hug!". I'm gonna end up destroying his temper, but it's always fun to make fun of him every now and then. He has funny reactions.

"What?! Hell nah," Aconite blushes even more and hits his breaking point, going back to the other room and laying himself down on my bed as usual. These two always bring the best out of me: Sometimes, I forget that I have chronic depression, and it's all thanks to them. To be frank, I'd be a dead woman long ago if they never showed up.

However, I can't stop thinking about that little girl. She reminded me a lot of myself when I was her age. I was starving constantly because my dad never let me eat anything. He'd usually sit at the dinner table with a buffet in front of him while I watch him devour it all. He would lock me up with chains and collars that was originally used for… "the rough stuff in the master bedroom". I don't like thinking about it, but he's the main reason for my trauma and how my chronic depression began to form itself. The insomnia crawled into my life like a sneaky spider right after my dad died. Passed away from illness. THANK. GOSH. After all that he's done to me, I ain't gonna be sad that he's gone. I was happy as could be when I heard the news from mom. I hoped I would be freed from the depression, as well as from him, but that didn't happen. After I got diagnosed with not only insomnia but also the chronic state in the depression, mom thought it'd be a good idea for me to become independent and build my own life. To try, at least.

Hasn't gone well so far, but my friends help me forget.

A few days go by without much happening. I've just been in my small apartment, looking for things to do. I've been continuing to write in the diary of course, and Azalea and Aconite are doing their best to help me with everyday life. My tongue still hurts though, but why is something I'm not remembering anymore. It slipped out of my brain completely, and every time I ask Azalea about it, she doesn't wanna tell me. She keeps saying it'll upset me, and she won't put me in such worry deliberately. I decide to go to Aconite for an answer. He's always upfront and honest, so why not?

"Hey, Aconite?"

"Yeah?"

"What happened with my tongue?"

"You don't remember? Damn, your memory sucks. Something like that would be stuck on my mind for some time."

"Please, tell me."

"No."

"What? Why?"

"Because Azalea told me not to tell you. I don't follow orders typically, but I don't want you to feel worse than you already feel, you know? We both know what you've been through."

"What I've been through… Wait, did I fall asleep and have a nightmare? A little girl; ring any bells?"

"… Shit," Aconite says, defeated. "Fine, I'll just tell you." And so, he explains everything to me, like I did to them. The more he goes on about the nightmare, the more I feel like I'll pass out for some reason. I just feel like my tongue will be ripped apart again, and I'll die from the blood's suffocation.

"Hey, you feelin' alright? You look kinda pale," Aconite makes the remark.

"Huh? No no, I'm okay. I'm thinking, that's all." I fail at reassuring him, because I can't even reassure myself. Why does this little girl bother me so damn much? I don't want to find out but my curiosity is getting the better off me. She's having some sort of heavy impact on my mind and soul too, apparently, since the last thing I see before actually passing out is Aconite and

Azalea running up to me and trying to grab me before I fall unconscious onto the cold floor.

I'm starting to regain consciousness and wake up, and once again, it's somewhere unfamiliar. Must be another dream. I hear Aconite's raw voice call me out while Azalea is crying. I shouldn't have worried them, but something just made me pass out. I remember feeling all dizzy after rehearing the nightmare story, but after that, I'm kind of lost. Azalea gasps when she sees me opening my sleepy eyes and hugs me tightly. It feels warm and soft. She smells lovely too.

Wait…

"WHY ARE YOU TWO HERE?! AND YOU'RE BOTH…"

"Real, flesh and blood and all. Yeah, I don't get it either, but something weird happened after you passed out: We passed out with you, as if, I dunno, following you into this creepy mansion," Aconite says, explaining the situation briefly to me. I stand up and look at them, observing every detail about them. They look back, awkwardly and shyly, while I'm pretty much staring them to death. I'm just trying to soak this in: Azalea and Aconite have never been in my dreams before, so I don't understand why they're here now. And why they're so vivid and realistic.

"Huh. So, my imaginary friends have come to life. Cool, yeah…" I feel like passing out a second time, out of confusion and happiness. I've always wanted them to be real, of course, so this is surreal, and this is coming from a gal who is not easily impressed or shocked. I reach out to touch their clothing, just for confirmation for my brain.

"Hey! Don't just touch us like that! I get it, you're surprised, but so are we. Let's just figure out a way from this place," Aconite embarrassingly says while quickly pulling away.

I turn to look at the scared Azalea. She looks so cute and little, a true beauty indeed. Aconite looks a bit more handsome and manly, but there's no way I'm telling him that. I decide to take Azalea's hand in mine, to make her sure of the fact that we're all together now and it'll be okay. She wipes her tears and nods affirmingly. Time to find an exit now!

We decide to explore the ancient-looking mansion. It's broken down everywhere, both in the floor, the walls and ceiling, but we try to navigate in the darkness anyways, since we couldn't stay in the room we woke up in forever, despite it being well-lit. Lots of rooms are big and plain empty; except for the disgusting bugs and spiderwebs. The more we look around, the more I understand that this is not a dream. It's reality, whether I like it or not. I'm stuck in a bad place with good friends at least... But why did we get sent here? I just don't get that part. Maybe I'll find out though.

"Exit!", Aconite exclaims while half-sprinting to the entrance door.

"Be careful, Aconite! There are cracks in the floor everywhere, you might fall!", Azalea makes a small scream, which he ignores. He checks the old door and return to us with bad news: Locked shut. Damn it.

"I don't understand anything…!", Azalea says, looking like she's about to cry again.

"Hmph. Crybaby," Aconite states.

"Stop, you two! We should keep our voices down. Who knows if we're the only ones here or not," I tell them with a scolding type of tone to my voice. As if it's a response to my statement, we start hearing… things. An elderly man laughing, a feminine voice crying, and the little girl! I recognize her among the voices! But she did say that she wouldn't help me, so I'd rather not call out for help. No one else does it; we're standing completely still, hands intertwined in fear. It feels like our lives are on the line, and if we move, we're going to die on the spot. I blink one time and a doll appears in front of me on the floor. The doll is slightly hidden beneath the cracks, but I did notice it. I pick it up and inspect it: It looks exactly like the little girl from the dream, but she has a broken heart sewed in on her chest. On her back, it's spelling out something. It's small text that's glowing in the dark.

"'Let's play Tag'," I say out loud in a quiet voice, almost like a whisper to the other two beside me.

"A game of Tag? What is this shit?", Aconite whispers back. "If we're gonna get killed, kill us in the most badass way possible!", he continues, trying to make the situation funny, but failing miserably at it.

"Stop. Swearing." He's like a wild animal sometimes, always going up and about with his dear swearwords. How it annoys me, especially when we're stuck in a mansion like this. He dismisses my 'order' and just tells us to continue walking, now that the voices have stopped, and we're surrounded by silence again.

"Should we try the second floor? The stairs seem weak, but…"

"… But let's do it!", Azalea gets interrupted by Aconite. Now that he's real, I can see how much of a pain in the ass he is. It's like he's trying to play the brave role, but I know he's scared inside. He can't hide anything from me, that guy.

We carefully take the stairs up to the second floor. It feels like the place just gets bigger and bigger. Like it's endless or something. Rooms everywhere to explore, one by one. We didn't even finish downstairs, and there's even a third floor! But at the same time, we might find some info in a study or a library. "If we wanna get out of here, let's look for as much information as possible. Think smart, not hard," I tell the two of them and they nod. I then ask a question I'm hoping they'll refuse, but it could help us in a way. "Should we split up...?"

"Hell. No. I'm staying by your side. Ain't no way I'm going alone. Besides, the crybaby would die right off the bat, falling in some hole somewhere or something," Aconite puts his arms behind his head and tries to sound confident, as usual.

Azalea is the type to take and accept other's criticism about her, so her flowery name really speaks for how gentle she actually is.

We go around, room after room, making sure we're not missing anything. No luck so far though. 'How long is this gonna go on?', I think to myself just as I hear Azalea in the room beside me gasp in shock. Sounds like she found something good! I hurry myself over, only to find ropes. Ropes hanging from the ceiling, neatly tied up and ready to be used. Covering up the walls are countless glowing notes and scribbles where it says things such as "DIE", "KILL YOURSELVES" and "GO TO HELL". In the rope hanging at the center of the room, there's a crumbled piece of paper. The paper itself is old, but the lettering is fresh and new. I reach for the paper and read out loud the words. It's my handwriting.

"A game of Tag. Succumb to Depression and you will lose. Don't get caught. If you do- "

"Why did you stop reading it?", Azalea hesitantly asks.

"Because there's a thick layer of dried blood covering the last bit," I respond, but before I have time to tell her that everything is written in my style, breathing is heard outside the door, in the hallway. Heavy breathing, getting closer and closer. Aconite covers both mine and Azalea's mouth with his big hands, barely letting us breathe. He looks frantically around the room, trying to find a good enough hiding spot. With time running out, he pushes us all into a corner where the person breathing shouldn't be able to find us. Azalea's tears are streaming quietly down Aconite's hands as we sit and wait for what's about to come in. Suddenly, a knock can be heard. When we don't get up and answer, the knocking gets aggressive, until the point where it's so loud that they're practically banging on the door in a motion that never stops. I squeeze Azalea's hand even harder and pray.

Something or someone finally barges in, making the door break and fly across the room. It's impossible to see in the dark, but the glow from the scribbles everywhere makes us see a hint of it. It's a black-and-white little girl, slightly hovering above the ground, with messy bangs covering her eyes. 'The little girl...!', I think to myself while being in shock that she's in here too. I know I heard her voice, but… why would she be here? And, more importantly, why's she after us? It sure as hell seems like it!

After just a couple of seconds, she turns around and 'hovers away'. Looks like her long bangs makes her eyesight bad. If it wasn't for that, we'd be goners already. When we don't hear her heavy breathing anymore, Aconite releases us from his grip, letting us sigh out in relief.

"It's the little girl… from my last dream…", I tell them while coughing a bit from the tension that was left, hanging on the ropes.

"H-how could that be? A dream is a dream, isn't it?", Azalea says in between sniffles.

"This is no dream. This is a nightmare," Aconite stands up and looks at the ropes for a minute, then at us. "I think I have an idea of what that thing is, but I won't say it yet. It feels too… unreal to be true. Anyway, let's go before it comes back."

The three of us look outside, and true enough, the little girl is gone. We aren't taking any chances though, so we only speak when absolutely necessary and make sure we're as quiet as possible as we walk down the long halls and the huge rooms. The tension is real, and it's gonna turn worse if the little girl comes back. Because of the mental exhaustion, we try to find a room with a bed so we all can take a slight break. A lock wouldn't be too bad either, so we can keep her out.

"How about this one?", I ask after finding a big bed in the middle of a room. There's not much else in there, but we really need to rest our bones, especially Azalea and Aconite. I mean, they did come to life for the first time, so...

We agree to take this room, even though it doesn't have a lock. Seems like the ways out are all tightly locked up but the rooms themselves doesn't have locks.

"Who's going to watch the door? Someone should, right?", Azalea says quietly, already frightened enough as it is. When no one answers, she tells us that we should take turns, and so we do. Azalea goes first, leaving me and Aconite in the room. We sit on each side of the dusty bed and make small talk as we rest.

"This place sure is creepy, huh? And we're getting nowhere," I start up the conversation.

"You really are a pessimist, ya know. But I kinda like that about you: You see it how you perceive it, and I agree that this world is pretty shit," he says while looking around, everywhere except at my face.

"Yeah." And now, of course, the awkward silence. We don't know what to say to each other, especially without Azalea's personality giving light to the room. Aconite lays down in the bed and keeps looking around with strange looks. Is he searching for something?

"Great; now you made it awkward," he accuses me.

"It's your fault too. It takes two to strike up a convo, and you're not being so helpful in here anyways," I harshly tell him. Ever since he's come to life, I've disliked him slightly. His attitude is awful. AWFUL. And I don't know if I want someone like that in my life forever.

"… Sorry."

"Hmm?"

"I'm sorry… for my behavior. This is embarrassing to admit, but I don't like myself that much, so all I can do is keep going forward. With Azalea and you," he speaks up, but in a softer and genuine tone. I've never heard him be like this, and I sure as hell never heard him apologize for something before.

"I guess even douchebags like you have a heart," I chuckle, starting my usual teasing. He takes it seriously though and takes my hand and puts it on his chest where his heart is located.

"I do have a heart. You can feel it, can't you?", Aconite tells me while looking into my eyes. What's gotten into him? Wait, what's gotten into me? My own heart is starting to race!

"I… I'm going to check on Azalea. It's time to switch," I tell Aconite while gently pulling back my hand. As I go, little do I know that Aconite is laying there in the bed, smiling and blushing from ear to ear, holding his hands as if to replicate the "moment" we just had. Azalea walks in and directly jumps up on the bed, getting close to Aconite.

"Well, well? How did it go?", she asks, having high expectations.

"I dunno…", he gives a vague response.

"Meh. I know you've loved her ever since we came into her life. Now that we are in this creepy place, in flesh and blood, it's a perfect time for a romantic confession!", Azalea tries to cheer him up. "I know you want to kiss her. You tried, right?"

"H-hey! I never said that! And I didn't do anything!", he gets red like a tomato from the things Azalea are whispering to him. "Sure, it's true, but why start something with her that will just disappear as soon as we get outta here? We're not even real."

"But for the moment, we are."

"… Just take a nap already. I'm sick of hearing your blabbering," Aconite dismisses the conversation, even though he knows Azalea has a valid point. Before she falls asleep in her cuddled position, he whispers a 'thanks' to her. Whether she heard it or not, he appreciates her like a little sister, after all.

I stare down the hallways, creeped out by the atmosphere. I hope Azalea and Aconite will be able to sleep, just a tiny bit. My stomach makes a sound. Hungry. Yeah, we've been in here for what seems like an eternity, so I'm not surprised that even I am getting carried away in needs and emotions. Conveniently enough, I did pass out with a protein bar in my pocket, so maybe we three could share it. Actually, I'm sure they need it more than I do: They just recently became real, as if they were reborn. They must have trouble discovering every single emotion existing.

In the middle of my thoughts, I hear the voices again. Three voices, all the same. I go towards the stair's ledge and look down. I see the little girl, hovering slowly up the stairs, clearly going for us. I run in to hastily wake up the sleeping ones.

"RUN!"

"What? Why?", they begin asking me before they hear the voices too, knowing it's the signal that the little girl is nearby.

We get out of the room and see her here on the second floor now. She's so incredibly slow, which gives us an advantage, but boy, she's creepy anyways. And according from the scribbles and notes in the other room, she cannot catch us under any circumstances. It gives me shivers thinking about what she would do to us. Azalea is very fragile though, and her leg gets caught in a small hole, giving her wood splinters on her foot.

"AHH!", a shriek is heard behind us.

"Azalea!", I scream while running back to her. The little girl is closing in on her, but I'm gonna do whatever it takes to help her. Luckily, I manage to drag her up from the hole in the floor, though it looks like she hurt her ankle. Hand in hand, we keep on running. Aconite finds a way for us to get down the stairs without running into the little girl, so we follow clumsily. Azalea is leaning on my shoulder while she's trying her best to get away. The more she moves, the deeper the splinters get, until they make drops of blood appear.

"I can't run anymore...", she comments hopelessly.

"Yes, You can! I'm not letting you get caught!", I encourage her, trying to make her move, but Aconite butts in and carries her up.

"Let's just go!", he says while running with the light-weight Azalea in his arms. I follow right away, and we manage to run long enough until we reach a dead end.

"Where do we go now?!", I panickily ask.

"How the fuck am I supposed to know?!", Aconite says, just as much in panic-mode. "Fuck, fuck, fuck... Think..."

And then, the voices stop. It's suspicious, since we just reached a dead end: Wouldn't it be best to take us on now?

"I ain't buying this," Aconite whispers roughly while looking around for the little girl. Nothing. Aconite let Azalea down on her feet, but just as he does so...

"ARGHHH!", she shrieks out in total pain. The little girl from before is bent down in an unnatural position, on all four, with her head twisted, biting down on the spot where Azalea hurt her lower leg. She is biting so hard that a visible, gigantic bite mark is starting to form.

"AZALEA!", me and Aconite scream in sync, trying to tear our friend from the little girl. Her monster-like teeth must hurt incredibly. Where did she even come from?! I look around and see that she came from the hole where Azalea fell in. Her mouth is constantly drooling, so a pool of drool has been following the drops of blood. I suppose that's how she found us so quickly, too.

"LET... HER... GO... YOU BITCH!", Aconite attacks the little girl by kicking her away with brute force. She flies all the way to the end of the hall, where we came from. Seemingly weak, she fades away while leaving behind a sobbing sound. Azalea, who clearly needs rest and medical attention, looks at us with a different look in her eyes. Her blue-green orbs are so deep, it feels like I'm staring into a well.

"How are you, Azalea?", I lean down to ask her gently.

"… We're never going to make it out of this place, are we?", she says while looking at her wound. She must be traumatized, since she gave such a pessimistic, out-of-character answer. She's always cheerful and has beautiful eyes that glimmers with hope, but those eyes are gone right now.

"Of course we are. Don't be stupid," Aconite says, trying to cheer her up in his own way. She doesn't respond though. Just looks at us with distance written all over her. Aconite and I don't know what to say anymore, as this is going nowhere, so we take her to the room with the dusty bed. Aconite lays her down while I tell her to sit still so I can remove the splinters properly and stop the bleeding. I used to self-harm a lot back in the day, so if there's something I'm knowledgeable about, it's wounds. I carefully take out the sharp pieces, one by one, and close the injury with a piece of her skirt that got caught up and teared off from all action.

"There ya go, all wrapped up! Do you feel better?", I say while smiling at Azalea the way she usually smiles at me.

"… No," she flatly replies.

"What's up with you? Damn, I'm sick of that shitty attitude," Aconite scolds her from across the room, standing near the door to keep watch.

"Says the one who has an actual shitty attitude," she whispers back, flat tone again. I'm a bit surprised, to be honest, since I've never heard Azalea ever swear or say anything bad about someone. Something has happened to her, most definitely. I just don't know what.

"Are you feeling alright, Azalea? You're not yourself," I decide to straight up ask her.

"I don't know. I feel empty, is all."

As soon as she said that, an aching appeared in my body. I can relate so much to how she's feeling, so I shouldn't be too hard on her… but I don't feel fully comfortable being in here right now, so I suggest to her that Aconite and I go search for a study or something of the sort nearby. Her response was a mere shrug, so we left.

"She's hella weird," Aconite makes a remark. He's absolutely right, but I don't want to speak bad about

Azalea, as I've been stuck with those kinds of thoughts myself, so I stay quiet.

While hearing the two go further away from her, Azalea stares up into the ceiling, looking at nothing. She doesn't know what happened, but she feels as if someone has ripped out her soul and put their own soul in her place. She's battling emotions she's never felt before: Anger, sadness, loneliness... everything and nothing, all at the same time. It's overwhelming, especially for her, who's extremely fragile in her ways of living. She hasn't even thought about death or dying once, but thoughts like that are slowly but surely forming themselves, engulfing her heart. She doesn't feel the pain in her deep leg wound, just emptiness.

"Hello," a sad voice tells the depressed Azalea. "Are you in pain?"

"Yes." Azalea doesn't say more than that. She doesn't care who's there, either. She just needs someone to talk to.

"Do you need help with the pain?", the voice continues.

"Yes," Azalea replies again.

"I can take your pain away."

"Really?", Azalea says, still not looking around for the owner of the voice.

"Yeah. We're friends now, aren't we?", the voice exclaims happily. Azalea decides to get up from the bed, and when she does so, she's suddenly in the room with the glowing scribbles on the walls... and the ropes. Difference is, there's only one rope in front of her now. And the little girl is there, stretching out her hand.

"Take my hand and you will never suffer again," she says with a smile, no eyes being shown. Azalea isn't moving on her own, yet she feels as if this was meant to happen. This is the way she was supposed to go, whether she liked it or not. She's hurting so much that the pain becomes empty-like, so she doesn't think anything or anyone matters at this point. Just as Azalea is about to take the little girl's hand, she hears someone running in, screaming her name desperately.

"AZALEA! DON'T DO IT!", me and Aconite yell from the top of our lungs.

"Stay back. It's her decision," the little girl threatens us and somehow makes our bodies freeze. We can't physically move anymore! We can't save Azalea! Only watch her make a move...

"I love you and Aconite. I truly do. And that's why I'm doing this," Azalea says with a smile and tears running down her rosy cheeks. She clings to what she believes is her fate and grabs the little girl's hand. When Azalea does so, her mind becomes muffled with a bunch of nothingness. She's completely oblivious to her surroundings and herself. The little girl is standing behind Azalea as she is preparing the rope that is waiting in front of her. She slowly places her head inside the noose, letting it sit comfortably there. The little girl occasionally lets out a giggle while her petite victim is seconds from her death. I cry while frozen in place, trying to speak and protest but my voice is gone too. Aconite stands with eyes wide open, in pure shock.

After a swift move, it's all over. Azalea's lifeless body swings back and forth. Her eyes are staring up into the ceiling. Her crooked head is completely pale from the suffocation, almost being blue. And that's when our bodies are released and we're able to move again. I immediately break down, while Aconite runs to Azalea and just stares, speechless. We can't believe we witnessed our friend's, our little sister's, own suicide like this.

Why?

Why?

Why?

"WHY!?", I shriek out in pure sadness. My tears continue to streak down my messy face. "I promised... that we'd grow old together...", I tell Azalea, who is dead right before my eyes. "So why did you leave us behind...?"

The little girl is still in the room, standing in the shadows with a grin on her face. She suddenly starts speaking, as if trying to make us go down with mere words.

"Why do you fight it?"

"Huh?", I look up to see the little girl looking down.

"I've taken everything she was and left a bitter taste in your mouth. You can't fight me nor plead with me. I take what I will and leave only that which you pray to God will leave you every time the sun sets. The pain... The longing... That stinging feeling in your heart that perhaps there was something you could have done. Once I've taken my fill and drained you dry, all you'll have is the endless reminder that time goes on... without her," the little girl says while gazing at her shoulder, back to where Azalea is hanging in the lethal rope.

"... Why do you do this?", I ask one final question before feeling like I'll pass out again.

"Because I must...", and that's the last thing I hear from the little girl before my eyes force themselves to close, and I collapse.

"Hey...! HEY...!", I hear a worried voice call out for me. My eyes are so dried out from all the tears, it's difficult to open them, but I recognize Aconite's voice. I'm half-awake, half-asleep, but I try my best to wake my body and mind up from the horrible nightmare I just went through. When I do manage to open my eyes, Aconite comments how sore and red they look. "Seems like you cried in your sleep, as well. Can't blame ya though."

"... What happened?", I ask Aconite. Even though I didn't want to hear it, I need confirmation that what just happened was not a dream within a dream.

"I... don't want to say it out loud. I just... can't."

"So, it wasn't a nightmare, huh..."

"No. The worst part is that this is reality," he says while looking down on the floor. It seems that he moved me to the bedroom while I was passed out. Yet... I feel an anger boiling up in me. I begin to tear up again, whispering in a frustrated tone to him. "Why didn't you do anything? Why didn't you save her?"

Aconite is taken aback that I'm angry at him, but right now, I'm just running on autopilot, spitting out whatever comes into my head.

"Why are you all mad at me? I did all I could!", he says, frustrated and confused.

"'All you could'? Yeah, clearly, since Azalea is fucking DEAD!", I scream, going out of control… but I don't have the time or the emotion to care at this point. Aconite looks at me angrily, and stabbed in the chest at the same time.

"… If you don't want me here right now, I'll go," he offered to give me some space, and God knows I need it.

"Get out. Now." My heart wants to tell him to not go, to be by my side, but my brain is telling me that I need time to reflect. And so, with slight hesitation, Aconite leaves me in the room and goes out, closing the door gently behind him.

Aconite goes down the halls, back and forth. He wants to give her time, but he knows himself and his temper too. He can't help but feel betrayed, by his friend and the one he loves. "This isn't the time to be thinking about feelings anyways," Aconite says out loud while deciding which way to go. He's got a fairly good idea of the map of the place, so maybe it wouldn't hurt to go as far as possible to cover even more?

"Third floor, it is," he tells himself with a deflective tone. He wants to brace himself for anything, but of course he is just as scared and frustrated as anyone else would be. Every step on the long staircase makes a loud creaking sound, creeping out Aconite more and more. He follows through though and gets to what looks like a giant attic. There is only one room in the place; the rest are dead insects, strands of empty ropes and spiderwebs. A glowing light is emitted from around the door to the separate room, making it very intriguing and curious.

"What is this?", Aconite says excitedly. "Hopefully something great is behind that door!" He runs to it and quickly opens it, revealing a white marble room. Occupying the walls are lights and plenty of bookshelves, while in the middle of the room is a bedside table with an hourglass on top. The hourglass looks very modern, compared to everything else in this forsaken mansion. Most of the contents are still on top, but there's some sand on the bottom, rolling down in a slow, real-life pace. For every minute that passes, a sand grain falls.

"I guess I'll read some books in here. That's better than being out there in the creepy ass hallways," Aconite says while looking on each shelf, trying to see if there's some useful info anywhere. "How about... this?" It's a smaller book, almost like a diary, that Aconite pulls out. The words don't glow this time around, and it looks unusually similar to Aconite's loved one's diary in the real world. He doesn't want to pry, but he has no choice, so he opens it up and realizes a weird thing. "Wait... this IS her diary! I recognize both the book and the handwriting. What the fuck is it doing here with us? Well... I might find something out if I read, so..."

After a few minutes of reading, he didn't find what he was personally looking for, unfortunately. He brings it with him anyways, to ironically show respect to the diary's owner. "Is there seriously nothing else interesting in these bookshelves? I'll look one last time before going back to her," Aconite murmurs to himself and sighs as he analyzes the shelves more. Most are children's books, but when he picks out a random one to read, another one falls on him, right on his head. "Ouch! What the fu- ", Aconite begins a complaining sentence but stops speaking to himself when he sees the cover of the book that fell down onto the floor. It's a completely black book with some sort of fading, white creature that's grinning while looking at its bleeding finger, not seeming to notice that it is also bleeding from the eye. It's a bizarre cover for a book, but that's what intrigues Aconite to pick it up and go through it. He leans on the wall while opening the first pages, and already being shocked by something. "Damn! I gotta show this to her! Right now!", he says out loud while running straight out of the attic room, hurrying down the stairs and trying to find his way back to his 'potential love'.

I'm trying to cool my anger down, but it's pretty hard when I feel so powerless. There was a moment where I felt like destroying everything in the room, but there are no things in here to begin with. It would feel so good, but I know it would hurt just as bad anyways. But I don't feel angry anymore. Angry is the wrong word for right now. Right now, I question myself with 'what if' scenarios. What if we had been quicker? What if all of us were smarter? What if neither of us ended up in this place? I know it's stupidly worthless, but I can't help to just want to escape from this pain. I tug my shirt at the spot where my heart is located, look up onto the ceiling and pray for the pain to go away. I don't know if it's God I'm praying to or just me muttering to myself... but if He is listening, please, help me.

A knock on the door scares me while I'm in the middle of my 'what if' questionings. "Aconite?", I whisper out, enough for the person who knocked to hear.

"Yeah. Can I come in?"

"Sure," I tell him without hesitating. I can't bear the pain anymore, and I need someone with a clear head with me.

"Hey! I found something that will amaze you!", he says while holding a strange-looking book.

"That creepy book you're holding, I assume?"

"It's creepy alright, but I've got so many clues for how to survive, and even better, getting outta here!", he says while smiling, teeth showing, but removes the smile from his face when he sees my expression and hears my next words.

"Can you revive people with it?"

"I mean, no, but..."

"There's no point in me reading it, then," I say while bringing my legs up to the bed, holding my kneecaps close to my chest, as if trying to make myself as small as possible. But Aconite reacts with rage, for some reason I don't understand.

"You're really pissing me off right now. I understand that the loss of Azalea was painful, almost too much, but does that mean we should follow her into death too? I sure as hell won't, and if you want to, I won't let you either!", he looks at me with angry looks in his eyes, but I know that he means well... somehow.

"I don't know... my mind is all cluttered, and I honestly just want to avoid the pain as much as possible."

"Then stop being a damn masochist and work with me! If you're not getting out of here for our sake, let's do it for Azalea!"

"... Fine, I'll take a look at the book. Sit beside me so you can explain it all."

As we go over the whole book, page by page, so many things make sense now. Even Azalea's death has an explanation to it, which lifts a small part of the gigantic pain from my heart. After finishing the book, Aconite puts it on the bed, and we start discussing it.

"So… we came here because I have unresolved traumas with my chronic depression? I… I'm sorry, Aconite. It's my fault."

"Don't say stupid stuff like that. You can't help what illness or diagnosis or whatever that you have. It's not like you willingly said that you wanted this," Aconite replies, trying to cheer me up as usual. To me, it always seemed like he was a liar, only acting tough in front of us, but I guess I turned a blind eye to the fact that he's actually pretty intelligent, rational and strong-willed. He's as real as can be.

"Whose fault is it then if it's not mine?"

"It's nobody's fault, but if you wanna blame someone, it would be the little girl, who we now know is your depression in a weird human-like monster form. The book did say that the monster that brought you in here is a reflection of your hidden feelings, after all. It explains why she tried to put you down more than me, since you two are one, technically. Remember the note where it said this is all 'a Game of Tag'? Guessing that none of us would do something like… that, I'm sure the little girl influences us somehow. I dunno, I'm just letting my thoughts speak, but I think I'm right."

"You're always right," I say with a hurting smile.

"You don't have to act differently around me. I can tell that you're sad behind that smile, you know," Aconite says while looking straight into my eyes. Caught.

"I'm sorry. I didn't mean for it to come off like that. I just... I'm starting to accept the situation and what happened with... yeah."

"Yeah, I know. That's why I'm going easy on ya. But know this: I'll always be here for you. I'm not planning on going anywhere. At least not without you," Aconite says while looking away again, but decides to be a man and say it while taking a hold of my hand. It's gentle, warm and full of life. That sense of comfort is what I need right now. We have a special kind of eye contact for a moment, just a moment, but it makes me realize that I can't afford losing him. Not because I already lost someone I regarded as a little sister, but because of him as an individual. My heart skips yet another beat, and I'm starting to understand why. Or rather, I think I'm starting to understand why, but I'm not 100% sure. I'm not going to focus on it so much now though. I just want to be able to grieve. To be able to cry and weep as much as I need to. I know this hole in my heart will never be replaced or heal, but when you lose someone, there comes eventually a time when the pain becomes bearable. I'm waiting for that time to arrive. Until then, I need to let myself be in denial, be angry, be having bargaining thoughts, be depressed, and feel acceptance... when I'm ready for it.

"A-anyway," Aconite says, breaking the eye contact, "at least now we know how this place works. Basically, the more fragile you are, the bigger risks there are that you won't make it. Your mentality is all that matters in here. Be strong in your head and heart at the same time and we should be able to get out. It sure explains Azalea's death... she was one hell of a cheery flower, always putting others before her."

"You don't have to put it like that, but... yes, she really was. I miss her."

"That makes two of us," Aconite says while sighing and laying himself down on the bed, arms crossed at the back of his head to support it. "There are some things this weird book didn't explain, like the sparkling attic room I mentioned, but little info is better than no info."

"Right," I give a short reply and lay myself down onto the bed as well. Slightly awkward silence fills the room like a fog, but then, Aconite speaks up.

"By the way, I found this too. Looks like your diary, so I brought it with me," he says while pulling out a smaller notebook. I recognize it right away.

"What?! What is my diary doing here?", I exclaim, snatching it out of Aconite's hands.

"Do you think I know, or something? Because I don't. I just randomly found it in one of the bookshelves in the attic, along with that creepy ass book," he says while pointing at where the book is. The thing is, it's not there anymore.

"What?", we both say at the same time. "Items can teleport too, now...?", I say in a complaining tone. "When is any of this going to end..."

Voices begin lurking in the dark. The usual voices that we're used to hearing when the little girl, the depression, places herself somewhere in the mansion. It's... kind of terrifying, not knowing where she's going to spawn next time.

"Oh, fucking fantastic," Aconite says with an irritated tone to his own voice, grabbing my hand forcefully and making us run out of the room and search for the little girl and a place to hide. I try to keep the book's words in my mind, telling myself over and over again to be strong, but it's not that easy. That's when I realize...

"Aconite? Is it just me or are the voices getting louder and more frequent?"

"Don't know, don't care. I'm looking out for our lives at the moment, not theirs!", he replies while looking frantically around. "Where the hell is she?! This is stressing me the fuck out!"

"You're the one stressing me out! Just find us a hiding place!", I say, annoyed at how much noise Aconite's always making. He stays silent from then on, but stops when we're about to go to the attic.

"Hello."

It's the little girl, blocking the stairway up to the mysterious room. Who knows why? All we know is that we need to proceed cautiously, or else it's over for both of us. I decide to take a different approach this time, which shocks Aconite. I breathe in deeply, through my nose, and let the air out through my mouth. Then, I turn to the little girl, and I kneel down to get at her level.

"Hello. How are you?", I greet her. This is a huge risk, and she could kill me at any moment, but I'm aware of that. I'm aware of everything, and I feel a sense of calm the more I look at the little girl. She's not actually intimidating or scary right now; she just feels lonely, in a way.

"I need help. Can you save me?"

I remember this. In that slender hallway, who knows how long ago. I didn't see it then, but now that I know that she's not only a little girl, but a part of me and who I am, I need to make sure I say what I want to say.

I only have once chance, and I'll be completely honest with myself. Whether the little girl accepts my answer or not, we'll see, but it is now or never that I can redeem myself and feel the acceptance that I've been chasing ever since my- no, our- dad did what he did to us.

"Do you want to hear a secret? I'll only tell you."

"What is it?", the little girl asks, looking up revealing her pale white eyes to me. I recognize those eyes. Those painfully sad eyes, filled with despair and nothing more.

"I will make sure that you never feel that pain again. Okay?", I say with a genuine smile. "I'll make sure you're never harmed. I'll take care of you. I want and need to be there for you, just like you've been there for me. All these years, suffering together… it's been tough, right?", and that's when I feel quiet tears streaming down my face.

"I just want to end it all sometimes. That's how much it hurts. Can you still save me?", the little girl asks for confirmation.

"Sure! I'll do whatever it takes. From now on, you will never feel like this. Instead, you will feel… hmm… what about 'happy'?"

"… What does 'happy' mean?", she asks me.

"Well… I'm not too sure myself, to be honest. But if I can give an example… I feel happy when I'm with you and you're with me!", I say, smiling once more to reassure her that I mean it. Depression shouldn't be seen as a curse; it should be seen as a gift to be out of the norm and not blend in with the crowd, thinking, doing and saying what everyone else does. When you learn what true pain is, you learn what true love is. I cannot believe I just realized it, but just like I want to be with Aconite, I want my depression to stay with me and help me grow into a healthier and stronger person. Someone that helps herself instead of ignoring their problems. Someone that can admit that they don't love everything about themselves and turn their weaknesses into strengths. Someone who can laugh at their unusual habits and quirks.

… Someone who can say 'It's okay to not feel okay'.

"Thank you. For saving me," the little girl replies. Seems like I said all my thoughts out loud without noticing, but it was for the best. I give the little girl a tight hug, letting my tears fall onto her tiny shoulder, while she's showing a smile that shows that she just learned what 'happy' means. As she fades away, I can feel myself slowly fading away too. I quickly turn to Aconite, worried about how it's going to be when we return to the real world. Up in the attic, the hourglass' last grain of sand just hit bottom and is now completely empty. The key was always solving herself.

"We're going back!", I tell him, but there's a bittersweet happiness in my voice. "But…"

"Don't say more. I'm going to start to cry, thinking about a life where I cannot be with you, either. Just watch from afar. Shit's gonna hurt, haha," Aconite says while looking at me with tears in his eyes but a warm smile on his face. "Just promise me you'll be happy from now on, with or without me."

"I promise. Thank you for being by my side for all these years and thank you for loving me when I couldn't love myself," I tell him, running to his side and reaching out my hand to touch him, one last time. But he is gone before I can do so.

"… I love you. And I love myself," are my final words before I wake up to the real world. I'm in my small apartment, messy as always. Aconite is nowhere near me. Somehow, I expected him to be able to go with me, but… I suppose that is too much to ask for.

"ACONITE!" I had to let out a scream. I promised myself I wouldn't be this frantic again, now that I'm at peace with who I am and what I have, but… I really thought WE would make it, not just I. I look around, searching for him. I'm in the kitchen, but I'm alone. I pick myself up as quickly and clumsily as I can, running to the other room. No one here either. Then I hear a snoring-like sound from the corner…

"Aconite! Wake up, please!", I try to grab a hold of him but I'm still going through his body, as if he was my imaginary friend again. Like nothing ever happened.

"Mmh… Oh, hey. Are we back?", he says after waking up on his own, looking lazily around.

"Don't you dare talk so casually about it! I almost wish we stayed in there for at least one more second so I could have held your hand one last time!", I tell him, spitting out word after word in his face. Not intentionally… I'm just feeling serene about how it ended.

"I mean… I know something better than holding hands," he says while going up from the bed, going straight towards me and doing something I never would've expected to be real, but it is. Our first kiss.

"What the fuck?!", I say after realizing we just kissed. "WHY AM I NOT GOING THROUGH YOU RIGHT NOW?"

"I don't know what you think, but I'm pretty satisfied."

"Don't be a pervert and answer my question!"

"I DON'T KNOW BUT I'M FUCKING HAPPY I GET TO TELL YOU AND SHOW YOU HOW MUCH I LOVE YOU", he screams at me. "Damn… you women are crazy sometimes…"

I stand still and silent for a second or two before bursting out in laughter.

"What? What's so damn funny now?", he says in his annoyed voice.

"Just shut up. I'm going to go get dressed up and we're going outside."

"Wait, what? Like on a…?"

"Yes! Now shush," I tell him while giving him a peck on the cheek before getting myself ready. After a minute, I find a simple but cute dress. No make up is needed. I'm going to be myself from now on. Nothing more, nothing less.

"Ready?", I ask him while holding the doorknob.

"Ready," he says, putting his hand over mine while we open the gate to our new life. Together.

Thank you, Azalea.